A Nickel, a Trolley, a Treasure House

by Sharon Reiss Baker   illustrated by Beth Peck

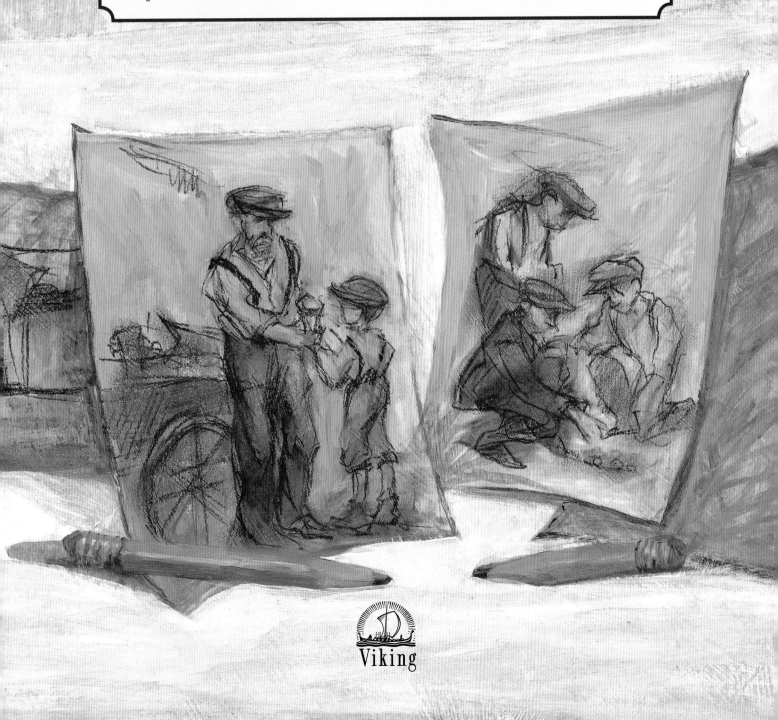

Viking

Long ago, before Lionel grew up and became an artist, he was a nine-year-old boy who lived in a tiny apartment on Ludlow Street. He had lived there ever since his family came from Poland to New York, and he knew every shopkeeper, every doorway, every sidewalk crack on his block.

Lionel's brothers delivered dresses for Mama's business. They sold hot chestnuts in the winter and ices in the summer. They shined shoes on the corner. Not Lionel. Drawing was what Lionel loved best. He spent all his spare time sketching on envelope backs and greengrocer lists. Such an odd habit, his mother whispered. Not much use for it, his father sighed. Perhaps he would outgrow it, they both agreed.

One spring morning, Lionel woke in the parlor, smelling the coffee his sister Rose had made before going to work at the dress shop. Mendel snored on the faded sofa. Reuben lay curled up on a mat on the floor. From the bedroom, Papa chanted his morning prayers.

When his brothers began to stir, Lionel reached for the little packet under the end of his cot mattress. Two pieces of gray cardboard, wrapped tightly with string, held a small stack of papers. He slipped it into the schoolbag beside him and fastened the buckles quickly.

Lionel's packet was a secret. Inside were his pictures, dozens of them. There was Joe the ice-cream peddler, holding out a paper cone to a penny-waving boy. There was the organ grinder with his monkey wearing the funny red cap. There was the storefront with the sign that read CIGARS FIVE CENTS.

Only two people knew about the packet. One was Rose, who had given him the cardboard and string from the dress shop. The other was Miss Morrissey, his teacher.

Miss Morrissey! Lionel suddenly remembered. Today he would ride on a trolley! He folded up his cot, spread the blanket over it neatly, and tiptoed into the kitchen, where he found the warm bowl of porridge Rose had left.

Only Rose knew about the trolley. He did not want to explain to the rest of the family how Miss Morrissey had caught sight of his packet and asked him to show it to her. She had studied his drawings for a long time. "Lionel," she said. "I see you protect these pictures quite carefully. But do you also show them to people?"

"Well, n-n-no," Lionel replied. He stopped, unsure of what to tell her. "I don't think anyone would care about them," he mumbled.

"I see," said Miss Morrissey. "I would like to take you on the trolley. Ask permission at home tonight, and then we'll go together after school tomorrow."

Alone in the kitchen, Lionel suddenly had a terrible thought. He did not have a nickel! He knew he needed a nickel to ride the trolley. The sign on the front of the trolley said PAY AS YOU ENTER. HAVE EXACT FARE READY. What would he do? He could not ask his brothers or Papa for the money. They would want to know why he needed it.

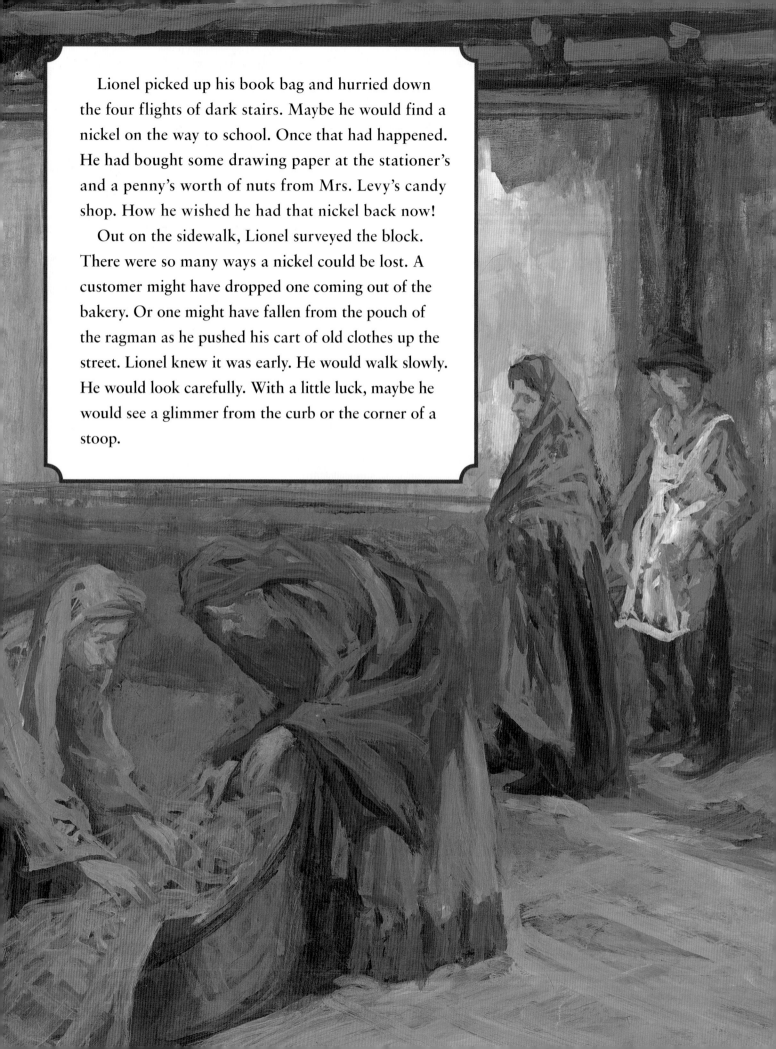

Lionel picked up his book bag and hurried down the four flights of dark stairs. Maybe he would find a nickel on the way to school. Once that had happened. He had bought some drawing paper at the stationer's and a penny's worth of nuts from Mrs. Levy's candy shop. How he wished he had that nickel back now!

Out on the sidewalk, Lionel surveyed the block. There were so many ways a nickel could be lost. A customer might have dropped one coming out of the bakery. Or one might have fallen from the pouch of the ragman as he pushed his cart of old clothes up the street. Lionel knew it was early. He would walk slowly. He would look carefully. With a little luck, maybe he would see a glimmer from the curb or the corner of a stoop.

Lionel's eyes scanned the streets and sidewalks all the way to the big brick school, but he found no nickel. What would he say to Miss Morrissey?

Lionel went to the boys' door and took his place in line behind Sammy Isaacs. A small group was seated on the pavement shooting marbles. Sammy turned around and noticed Lionel.

"Hiya, Lionel," he said, pointing at a clear marble with blossoming green swirls inside. "Wouldja look at that! Irv's got a new cat's-eye shooter." Lionel enjoyed watching the boys play. Hunched over, their shadows touching on the sidewalk, they made an interesting sight.

"Hey, Lionel," Sammy said. "How come you're so dressed up today?"

"Aww, they're just my old knickers." Lionel tried to brush off the question.

"Yeah, but you look so—I dunno, ready for Shabbos or somethin'."

Lionel didn't reply. Then the bell rang, sending the marble shooters scurrying for their places.

Lionel followed Sammy to the classroom. *Nickel, nickel, nickel,* he worried to himself with each step. Suddenly a happy thought occurred to him. Perhaps children could ride free!

On most days, Lionel enjoyed school. Today, though, it was hard for him to concentrate. He tried to sit still, but he felt wriggly inside, wondering where his teacher would take him.

When the bell finally rang, he followed Miss Morrissey out to the warm, sunny street.

"What an adventure we will have this afternoon, Lionel," Miss Morrissey said as they crossed Canal Street. "I have not been to the museum in quite a long time, and I am so looking forward to it."

The museum! Lionel did not know exactly what a museum was, but he felt a small shiver go through him at the grandeur of the word. So that was where they were going!

Just after the pair reached Delancey, a bright yellow trolley swayed down the street and stopped in front of them. "Step right up, son," boomed the conductor. So Lionel mounted the big black step in front of him, pushed open a small iron gate, and found himself eye-level with a tall wooden box. Over an arched window on the front of the box was a small white sign that said in black letters FARE 5¢.

It said nothing about children riding free. Lionel felt his face go hot. How silly he had been. Of course such a wonderful thing as a trolley ride must cost the same for everyone. Now the conductor would ask him to get off. He would not have a chance to ride, he would not find out what a museum was, and Miss Morrissey would have wasted her time with him.

Suddenly two shiny nickels tumbled down behind the glass, then dropped out of sight at the bottom. Two nickels—Miss Morrissey had paid a double fare!

"Miss Morrissey," Lionel began, "I'm sorry I don't have a nickel today. Maybe I could pay you back. . . ."

"Pay me back?" echoed Miss Morrissey. "On the contrary, dear Lionel, it is my privilege to accompany you on this expedition. I could never dream of accepting any reimbursement."

Lionel did not understand all her elegant words, but he did understand that she meant to pay his fare. The trolley clattered beneath Lionel's feet as he followed her and took a seat.

He watched the familiar shops and buildings fly by. At the Bowery, the noisy street that was the neighborhood boundary, the conductor called out, "Transfer here for uptown."

"Two rides for the price of one." Miss Morrissey smiled at Lionel as they settled in to a second trolley. But Lionel was staring out the window. He had never traveled outside his neighborhood before, at least not since he first came to America. They were just a few blocks away, and yet already his home, school, the stores and people he knew had disappeared. The city seemed to have swallowed them up.

Miss Morrissey was watching him. "Lionel," she said softly, "it can be scary to leave your own neighborhood—thrilling, of course, to see the world, but scary, too."

"Yes," said Lionel, and wondered how she knew.

Lionel tried to imagine what happened in museums. Perhaps there was some kind of show, like the musical review Rose had once seen. But, no, that did not seem right. More likely, there was an assembly like in school. He would need to sit quietly and listen to someone talk.

"Seventy-Ninth Street!" called the conductor.
Lionel jumped up to follow Miss Morrissey
off the trolley. When they had walked a few
blocks down the quiet sidewalks, Lionel was
amazed to find himself across the street from
a large white palace. At least, it looked like a
palace, one of those majestic buildings in his
schoolbooks.

"Where are we?" he asked, bewildered.

"Why, Lionel," Miss Morrissey replied, "we
have arrived at our destination! This"—and she
gestured broadly toward the building—"this is
the Metropolitan Museum of Art!"

"Does someone live here?" Lionel asked.
"Someone important?"

Miss Morrissey looked surprised. "No,
Lionel," she began. "Well, perhaps in a way.
Come inside and see."

The museum was cool and dark after the bright
sun outdoors. Lionel blinked and then stared.
Overhead was a rounded ceiling so high that
Lionel felt very small. Men in crisp suits and ladies
in rustling silks strolled by him, talking softly.
Lionel smoothed his knickers. They did not look as
pressed as they had that morning.

He followed Miss Morrissey across the polished
stone floors into a large room. It was empty except
for a few benches facing the walls. How strange,
thought Lionel, to have such a grand room without
anything in it.

Then he noticed the paintings. They hung in
lines on the walls, each one framed in gold or dark
wood. Big pictures, bigger even than Lionel or
Miss Morrissey. Tiny pictures. Square pictures.
Rectangular and even oval pictures. He wanted to
walk right up for a closer look, but he thought it
might not be polite.

"You may look as much as you wish, Lionel,"
Miss Morrissey said. "That is why we have come."

So that is why we have come. Lionel felt his
mouth form an astonished O.

It was hard to know where to start. A path through snowy woods in one frame caught Lionel's eye. The snow was so clean and pure, not like the crackly gray ice that covered the New York sidewalks in winter.

He stopped in front of another, bigger picture and held back a laugh. A life-sized cat, perched on an overturned box, pawed greedily at a pile of fish around him. He had the same guilty look as Blacky, the cat who stalked the fishmonger on Lionel's block. "Thief!" Lionel could almost hear the fishmonger hiss. "Scat!"

Lionel's stomach flip-flopped when he read the brass plaque hanging under the next picture. *Interior of a Gothic Church.* No one in Lionel's family had ever been inside a church. He hoped it was all right to look at one hanging on a wall. He admired the pointy arches rising from the diamond-patterned floor to the ceiling. Maybe St. Theresa's, down on East Broadway, looked like this inside.

Standing close to another painting, Lionel felt confused. It seemed to be a picture of nothing at all, just lumps, flakes, and bumpy clots of paint.

"Step back, Lionel," Miss Morrissey said. He did and suddenly saw a long-haired man wearing a cloak that glistened in the light. "A technique the master Rembrandt taught to his students," Miss Morrissey explained. "He used a special knife to work the paint over the surface." Lionel moved forward and back, watching the man appear and disappear into the canvas. *Where did Rembrandt get that thick paint?* Lionel wondered. He had never seen anything like it at the stationer's.

They joined a few people in front of a picture of a thin, blond boy holding a sword. The sword looked too long for him, and Lionel thought it must be very heavy. He wondered how the boy had gotten that sword and if he ever used it.

"Who is that boy, Miss Morrissey?"

"He must be someone the artist knew," she answered. "He looks rather tired, don't you think? Sometimes artists like to have people dress up to have their pictures painted. But I think that boy was ready to go outside to play marbles or stickball!"

"Miss Morrissey," Lionel began in a low voice. "About the other people, why do they come to look at the pictures? I mean, what use do they have for them?"

Miss Morrissey looked back at the picture of the boy and answered almost as if she had not heard him. "The artist who painted this boy was Manet, a Frenchman who died about twenty years ago. Just think, Lionel, this young boy in the painting must be grown up by now, maybe with children of his own." She paused. "But we can always come here to see him as he was back then, as Manet saw him. That is why people come to the museum, Lionel, to see the world through the artists' eyes."

When it was time to go, the two made their way back to the trolley stop. The afternoon light had softened, giving the buildings a warm, rosy glow. Lionel felt sleepy as he took his seat on the bench. Shiny nickels, he thought drowsily. Transfer tickets. A trip across the city. A palace—no, better, a museum with pictures. What a day it had been.

The buildings were closer together now and a familiar gray. Down the Bowery to Delancey Street. Another transfer. Swaying and clacking, the trolley brought them home.

It was still light after supper that evening. Lionel took his pencil, a sheet of Rose's dress-pattern paper, and his special packet down the block. Sammy, Irv, and some other boys were back outside with their marbles. Lionel sat on a stoop near them and began to draw. He liked the feeling in his fingers as the pencil scritch-scratched across the paper.

"Where were ya goin' after school with Miss Morrissey?" Sammy called to him.

"She took me to see a museum," answered Lionel.

"A museum? No kidding!" Sammy's eyes grew wide. "I kind of forget what that is, though."

"Well," said Lionel, "outside it's like a palace, same as the pictures in our books. But inside it's full of paintings and drawings from all kinds of places. People can go in and look all they want."

Sammy thought for a moment. He came closer and peered at Lionel's drawing. "Hey, Lionel, that's pretty good! You got Irv just right, scrunched over that marble. Don't forget to put me in the picture, too," he yelled as he dashed back to the game and plopped down. "Hey, Irv," he shouted. "Whadda ya think? You and me and all the guys—we're gonna be in Lionel's picture. It'll be in the museum palace one day." He crouched low, lining up a shot, then shouted, "An' everyone in New York will come and see just how we look now. Isn't that right, Lionel?"

Lionel smiled as he sketched Sammy's fingers curling around a marble. There was nothing he liked better than sitting on the stoop, drawing the people he knew in the place he knew best.

"Could be, Sammy," he called back. "It just could be."

Author's Note

Some people, knowing that my grandpa Lionel was an artist from New York, have asked whether this is a true story. A few family details are factual. For example, Lionel's sister Rose really did work in a dress shop. The rest of the book grew out of something my grandfather told me over and over when I was little: a teacher changed his life by paying his trolley fare and taking him to the Metropolitan Museum of Art. That was all I knew, and since Grandpa Lionel died years before I wrote this book, I relied on research and imagination to tell the rest. I modeled some characters on people I know. Miss Morrissey may seem familiar to students of one of South Florida's best teachers, Ms. Paula Cochrane.

In describing Lionel's world, I wanted to be historically accurate. I toured his old neighborhood with a historian, visited the Tenement Museum to see what his apartment might have looked like, and went to the Transit Museum in Brooklyn to study old trolleys. I also researched which paintings the Metropolitan Museum of Art owned in the early 1900s, and I included some of them in these pages. For the art-curious among you, they are, in order of appearance, Barend Cornelis Koekkoek's *Winter Landscape, Holland*, Giuseppe Recco's *A Cat Stealing Fish*, Pieter Neeffs the Elder's *Interior of a Gothic Church*, an unknown artist's *Man with a Beard* (in the style of Rembrandt), and Édouard Manet's *Boy with a Sword*.

For Matthew, Rachel, and Noa Baker
and Isaac and Sophie Reiss —SRB

For Beth and Ari
(in honor and memory of Bob) with love —BP

VIKING
Published by Penguin Group
Penguin Young Readers Group, 345 Hudson Street, New York, New York 10014, U.S.A.
Penguin Books Ltd, Registered Offices: 80 Strand, London WC2R 0RL, England

First published in 2007 by Viking, a division of Penguin Young Readers Group

1 3 5 7 9 10 8 6 4 2

Text copyright © Sharon Reiss Baker, 2007
Illustrations copyright © Beth Peck, 2007
All rights reserved

LIBRARY OF CONGRESS CATALOGING-IN-PUBLICATION DATA IS AVAILABLE
ISBN 978-0-670-05982-9

Set in Sabon MT semi bold   Book design by Jim Hoover   Manufactured in China